The White Nights of Ramadan

The White Nights of Ramadan

Maha Addasi

Illustrated by Ned Gannon

BOYDS MILLS PRESS

AN IMPRINT OF HIGHLIGHTS • HONESDALE, PENNSYLVANIA

To my mom and dad—"I walked and walked."
—MA

For Kathleen, who helped me appreciate the value of cultural history
—NG

The author wishes to thank Shurooq Amin, Ph.D.,
Kuwait University, for her assistance.

Text copyright © 2008 by Maha Addasi
Illustrations copyright © 2008 by Ned Gannon
All rights reserved.
For information about permission to reproduce selections from this book,
please contact permissions@highlights.com.

Boyds Mills Press
An Imprint of Highlights
815 Church Street
Honesdale, Pennsylvania 18431
Printed in China

Library of Congress Cataloging-in-Publication Data

Addasi, Maha.
The white nights of Ramadan / Maha Addasi ; illustrated by Ned Gannon.
p. cm.

ISBN 978-1-59078-523-2 (hc) • ISBN 978-1-62979-846-2 (p)
1. Ramadan—Juvenile literature. 2. Fasts and feasts—Islam—Juvenile literature.
3. Islam—Customs and practices—Juvenile literature. I. Gannon, Ned. II. Title.

BP186.4.A25 2008
297.3'62—dc22
2008002637

First paperback edition, 2017
The text of this book is set in Caxton.
The illustrations are done in oils.
10 9 8 7 6 5 4 3 2 1

Noor stared out her bedroom window at the rising moon. "It's almost time," she whispered and ran to tell her brothers.

"Look out the window!" Noor said. "The moon is almost full. The middle of Ramadan will soon be here."

"And *Girgian*!" said Sam.

"Yes, and Girgian," said Noor.

Sam and Dan smacked their hands in a high five and sang, "Girgian! O Girgian! Candy! O candy!"

"Look! I'm a *musaher*," said Sam, banging his drum.

The musaher walked through their neighborhood before dawn, beating his drum to wake people up for the *suhoor* meal. Sometimes the musaher even left gifts.

"Well, my musaher," said Noor, "we'd better get busy and make the candy."

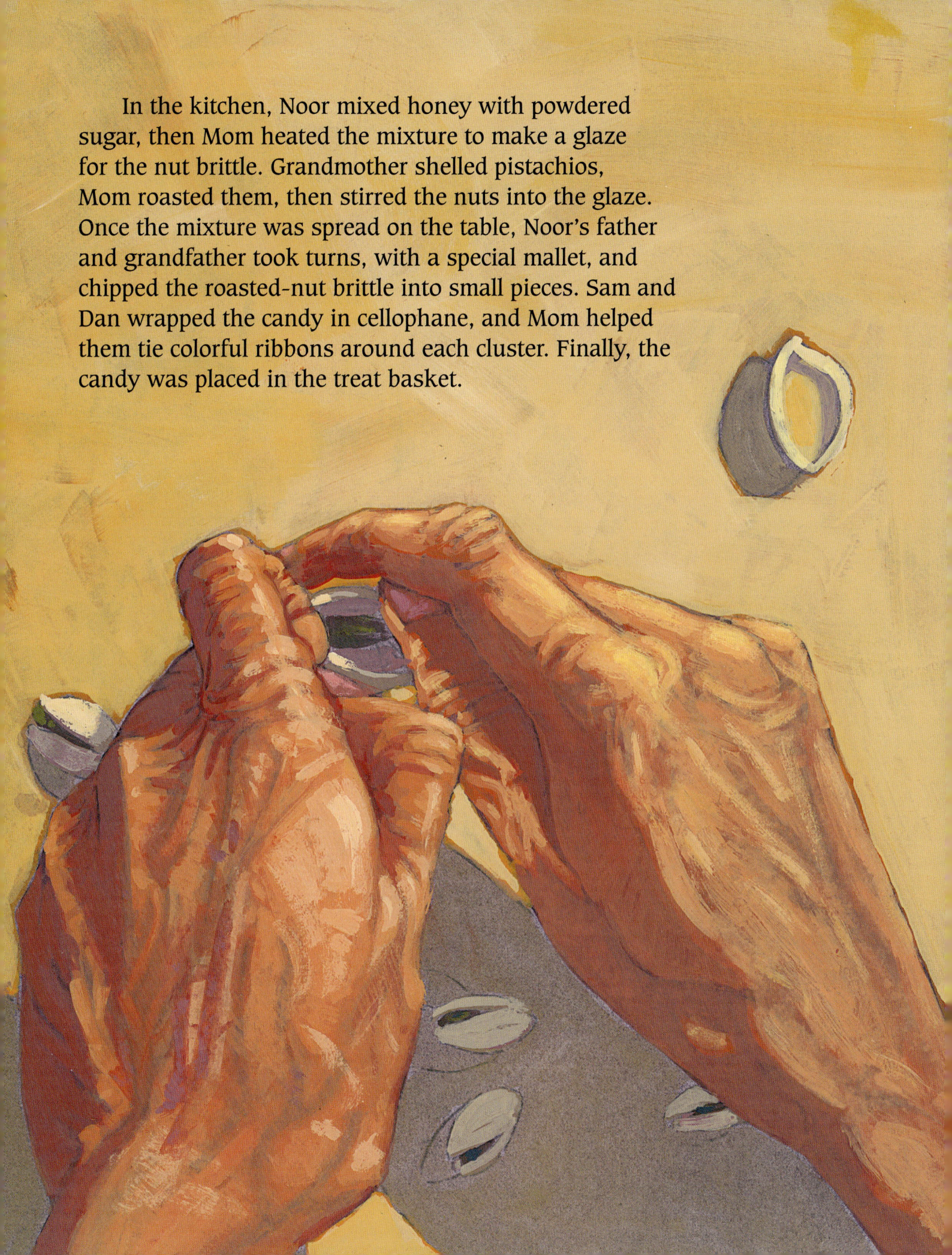

In the kitchen, Noor mixed honey with powdered sugar, then Mom heated the mixture to make a glaze for the nut brittle. Grandmother shelled pistachios, Mom roasted them, then stirred the nuts into the glaze. Once the mixture was spread on the table, Noor's father and grandfather took turns, with a special mallet, and chipped the roasted-nut brittle into small pieces. Sam and Dan wrapped the candy in cellophane, and Mom helped them tie colorful ribbons around each cluster. Finally, the candy was placed in the treat basket.

"Now we must decorate the bags," said Noor. "Beautiful bags mean more candy!"

Noor and her brothers painted their canvas bags with bright colors. When the bags were dry, they glued colorful beads on them. Then Noor threaded yellow ribbon through the slits at the top of Dan's bag and tied it around his waist.

"I'll take green ribbons!" Sam said.

For her own bag, Noor chose ribbons of red and gold, her favorite colors. Then it was time to try on her fancy dress.

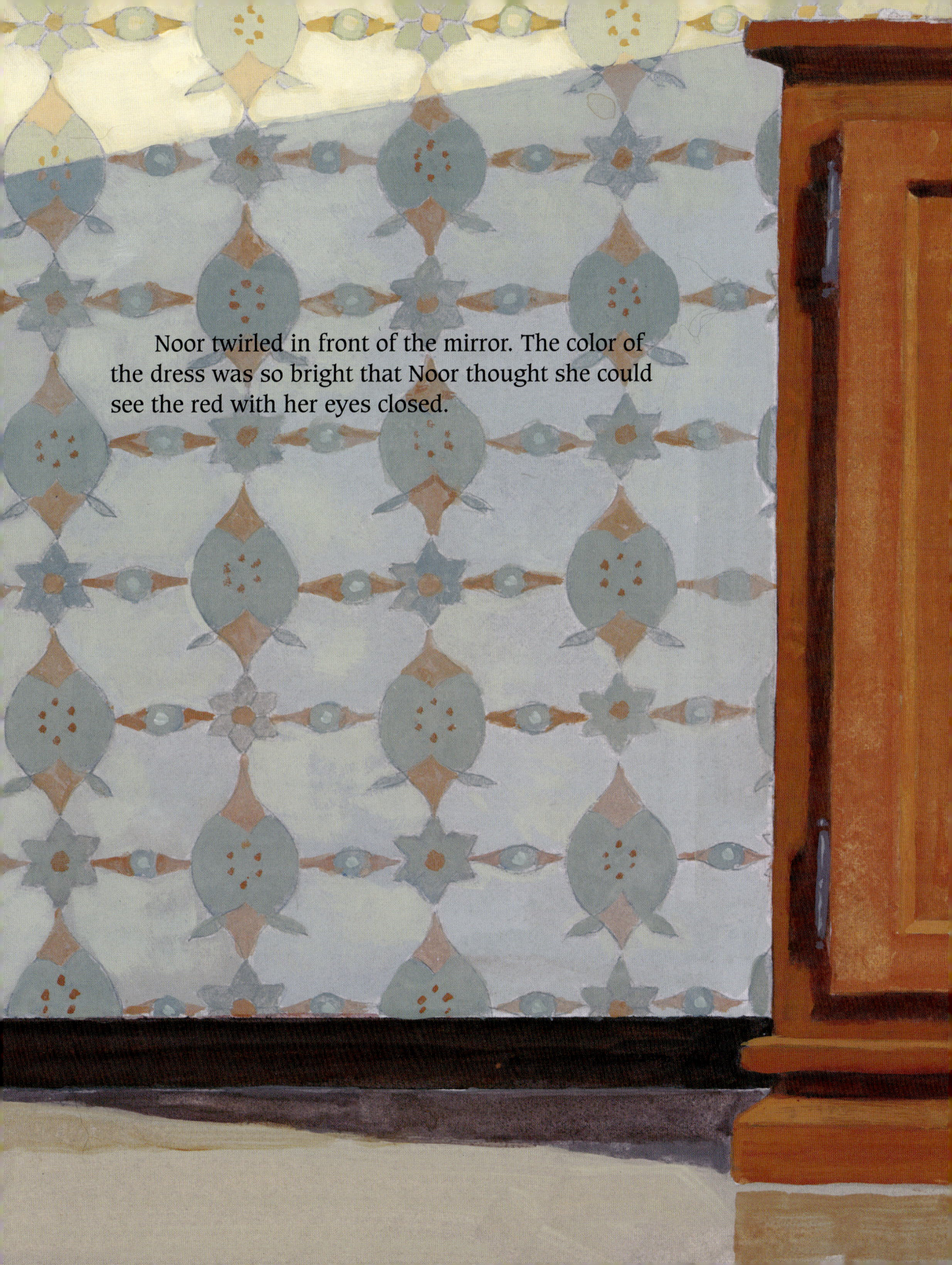

Noor twirled in front of the mirror. The color of the dress was so bright that Noor thought she could see the red with her eyes closed.

That night, Noor was too excited to sleep. She kept checking the candy and the *fanouses*, special Ramadan lanterns that would light up their path for Girgian. No one needed a musaher that night; the whole family was up well before dawn.

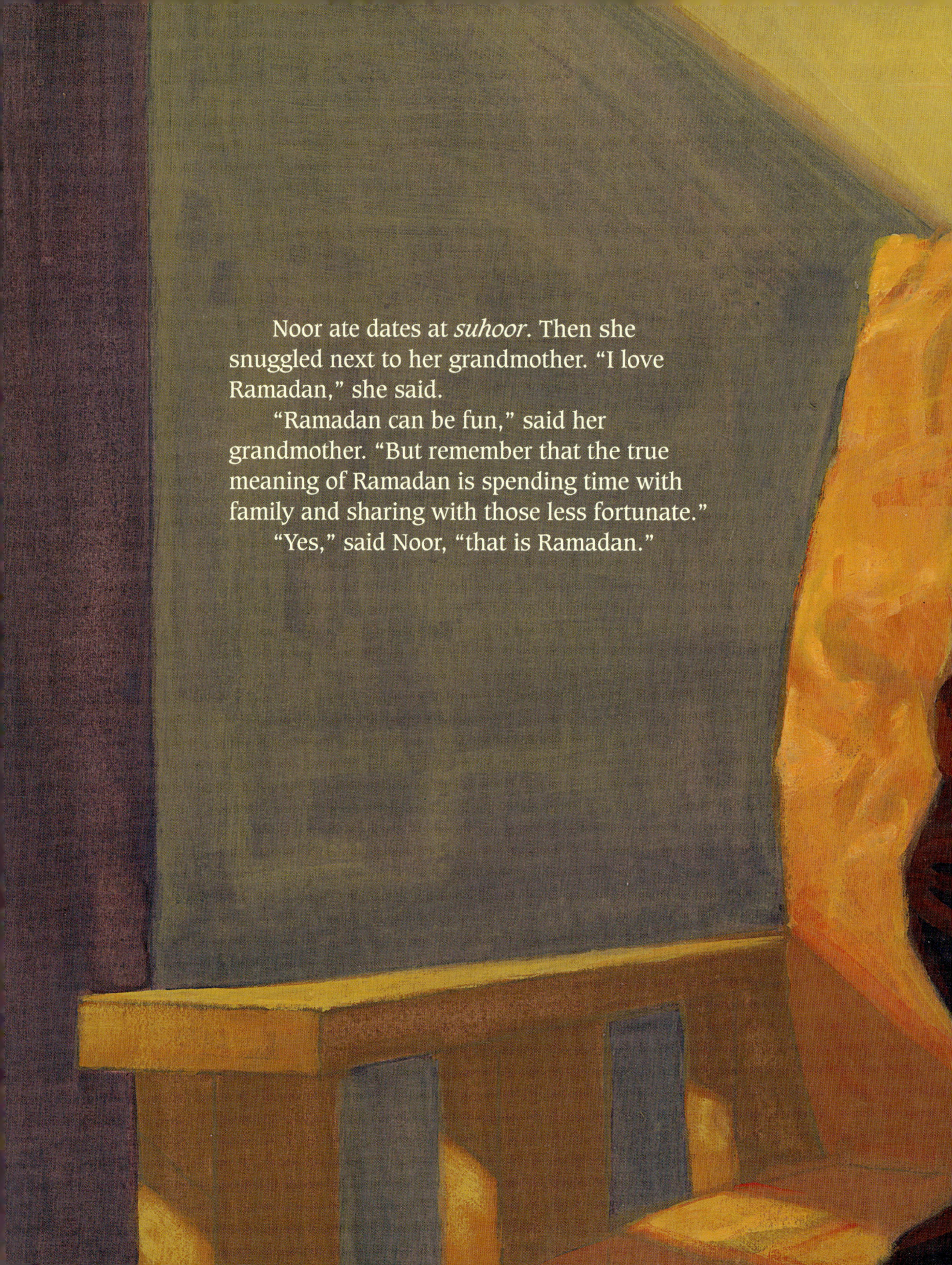

Noor ate dates at *suhoor*. Then she snuggled next to her grandmother. "I love Ramadan," she said.

"Ramadan can be fun," said her grandmother. "But remember that the true meaning of Ramadan is spending time with family and sharing with those less fortunate."

"Yes," said Noor, "that is Ramadan."

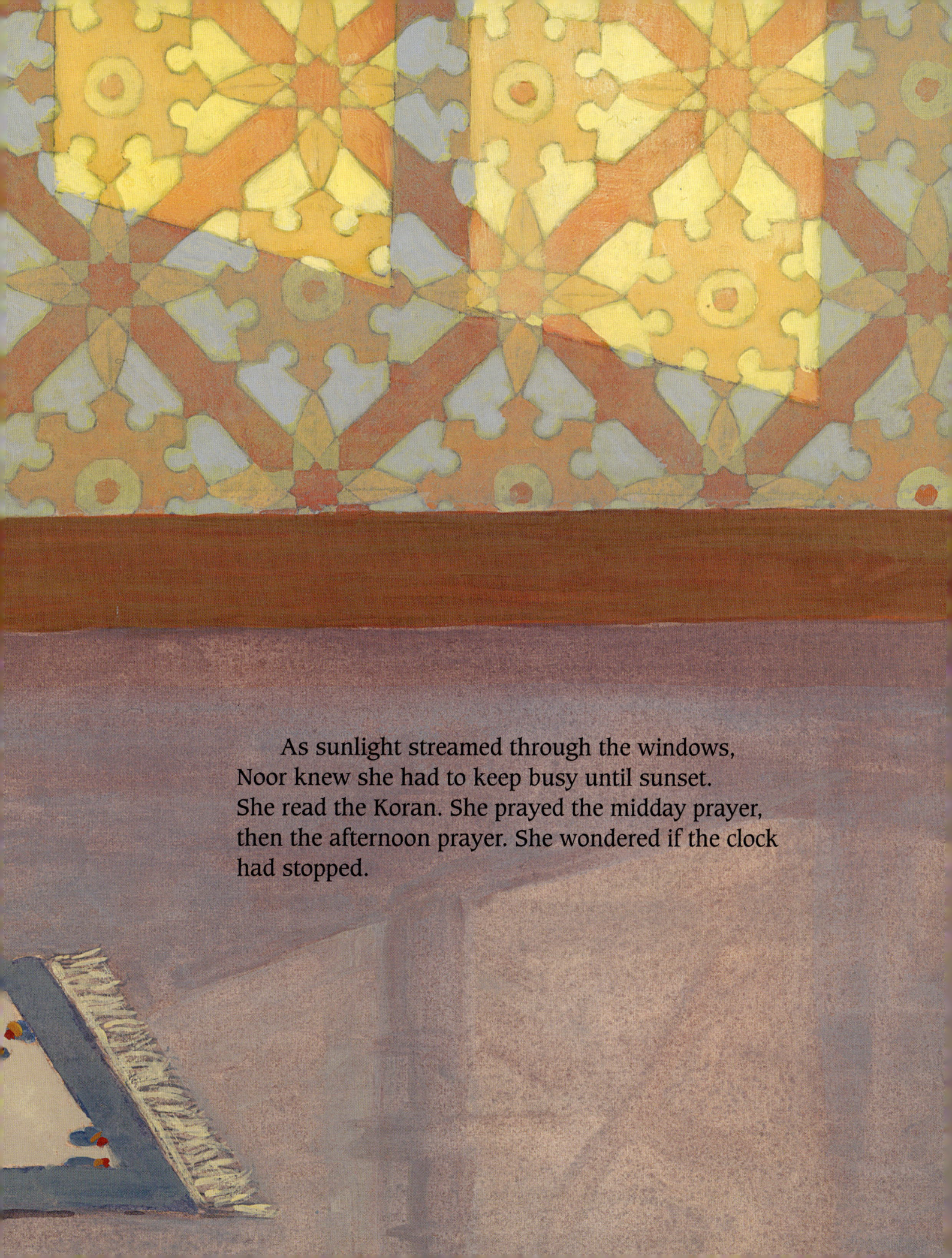

As sunlight streamed through the windows, Noor knew she had to keep busy until sunset. She read the Koran. She prayed the midday prayer, then the afternoon prayer. She wondered if the clock had stopped.

Finally, the sun set and Noor joined her family to break her fast at *iftar*. She had not had anything to eat or drink since suhoor. Sam and Dan, who were too young to fast, finished eating quickly.

After iftar, Noor and her brothers got ready. Sam and Dan dressed in their traditional *dishdashas*. "You look very handsome," said their grandmother.

Then Noor came down the stairs wearing her fancy dress.

"You look beautiful!" said her mother.

Noor's heart beat as fast as the drums of the musaher himself as she held up her brass fanous. Dad snapped many pictures. Noor and her brothers tied their bags in place, and with Grandfather by their side, they went on their Girgian walk.

Everywhere she looked, Noor saw children in shimmering costumes. She heard singing throughout the neighborhood. Colorful fanouses lit the night. *It's no wonder that the middle days of the month are known as the "three whites,"* Noor thought. With the full moon in the sky, it all made sense to her now. She decided that Girgian should be called the "white nights of Ramadan."

Dan knocked at the first door, and Sam, who had insisted on strapping his drum around his neck, stood at attention. When the neighbor opened the door, Noor and Dan sang, "Girgian! O Girgian!"

Sam beat his drum. "I'm the new musaher," he announced. The neighbor laughed and dropped candy in their bags.

By the end of the night, the crinkly cellophane stuck out of their candy bags like flowers in a vase.

"I'll be musaher for two more nights!" Sam said.

When Noor and her brothers returned home with their sweet treasures, their mother was waiting with a food basket for the poor. "Now comes the time for sharing," she said and handed the basket to Noor.

As Noor and her grandfather walked to the *mosque* to deliver the basket, she remembered what her grandmother had said about Ramadan. She took her grandfather's hand and turned her eyes to the sky.

"Look at the Ramadan moon, Grandpa," Noor said. "Isn't it beautiful?"

"It certainly is beautiful, my Noor," her grandfather said. "It certainly is."

Author's Note

Observant, able Muslims fast during the daylight hours of the entire ninth month of their calendar year. This month is called Ramadan. During the fast, Muslims abstain from food and drink. Families have a meal before dawn called *suhoor*. Children join in that meal even if they are not fasting. (The elderly, pregnant women, the ill, and children are not required to fast.) Eventually, as children get older, they start fasting for one or two days of the month to practice.

Traditionally, families in the Middle East are woken by a man called the *musaher*, who walks through neighborhoods beating a drum and calling out to people to get up for suhoor. People start the fast a few minutes before the *muezzin* (moo-EZ-in) calls for prayers in the predawn. During the day, people read the holy book, the Koran. Muslims believe that the Koran was first revealed in this month. After the sun sets completely, families have a meal called the *iftar*, which means "breaking of the fast." Traditionally, Muslims start this meal by eating some dates.

Ramadan is supposed to place Muslims on equal footing with the poor and underprivileged. Almsgiving, *zakat*, is encouraged year-round, as it is a pillar of the faith, but during Ramadan, Muslims offer special alms called *zakat-il-fitr*. This consists of food or money or both.

In the countries of the Arabian Sea–Persian Gulf region, such as Oman, Qatar, Saudi Arabia, Bahrain, the United Arab Emirates, and Kuwait, where I was born and raised and where this story takes place, Muslims have a special celebration in the middle of the month. It is known as *Girgian* in Kuwait, *Gargaoun* in Bahrain, and *Garangaou* in Qatar. Each of these words means "sweets" or "candy" in their respective dialects. They all come from the same root word *garga'a*, which in the Arabian Gulf dialect is the word for the sound of hard candy rattling in a bag. For three consecutive nights, children wear traditional clothes, tie fancy bags to their waists, and carry lanterns to collect treats from neighbors, just like trick-or-treating. The Girgian treats are often roasted-nut brittle or store-bought candy. Although Girgian lasts for three nights, extended family members visit each other throughout the month, and families offer sweets like *atayef*, deep fried, pecan-stuffed pancakes doused in syrup.

In Egypt, there is a similar ritual in the beginning of the month in which children swing their lanterns, collect candy, and sing "Wahawi Ya Wahawi," a traditional song about the advent of Ramadan.

Glossary

Dishdasha (dish-DA-sha) An outfit worn by boys and men in the Arabian Gulf countries. It looks like a collared white shirt or tunic, but reaches all the way to the floor.

Fanous The Arabic word for "lantern." Though not a part of Ramadan ritual, the fanous is a traditional Ramadan home decoration in the Middle East. The origin of the Ramadan fanous is unclear, but some believe that the tradition began in Egypt, where lanterns were hoisted to the tops of minarets as a sign to people that the sun had set completely and that the day's fast was over. Today these lanterns are popular during Ramadan in all Middle Eastern countries.

Girgian (gur-gee-ANN) A celebration, observed mostly in the Arabian Gulf states, that takes place in the middle of the month of Ramadan, when the moon is full. In Kuwait, it lasts for three consecutive nights.

Iftar The meal for breaking the fast each day during Ramadan at sunset, when the whole disk of the sun disappears under the horizon. *Iftar* literally means "breaking the fast."

Koran (or Quran) The holy book for Muslims.

Mosque (or Masjid) The place of worship for Muslims. The building usually has one dome and a high towerlike minaret.

Musaher An Arabic word for a man who traditionally comes through neighborhoods in Middle Eastern countries beating loudly on drums to wake people up for the predawn meal. The musaher was important during the days before alarm clocks, and although he has been phased out from some neighborhoods, he is still a part of Ramadan tradition.

Noor A name for girls and sometimes boys, too. It means "light" or "guiding light."

Ramadan The ninth month of the Muslim calendar year. Muslims abstain from food and drink from a little before dawn until sundown each day during that month. The month begins when the first sliver of a crescent moon, after the new moon, is seen.

Suhoor The meal that takes place before dawn during the month of Ramadan. Children, even when they are too young to fast, join the family at suhoor. (Both musaher and suhoor come from the same root word—*sahar*, which means "before daybreak.")

The "Three Whites" The Islamic calendar is lunar, which means it is based on the phases of the moon. The middle of each month is marked by the full moon. The day before the full moon, the day of the full moon, and the day after are referred to as the "three whites." During Ramadan, the "three whites" coincide with the traditional time for Girgian.